Fun on t'

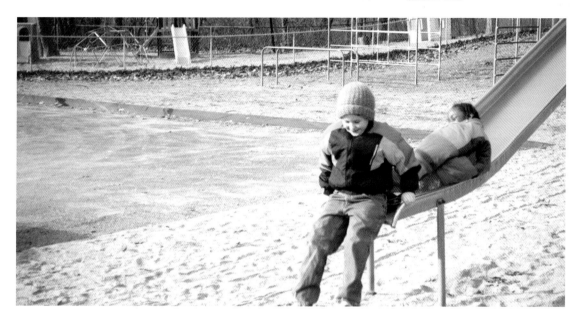

by
Laurel Dickey

Pioneer Valley Educational Press, Inc.

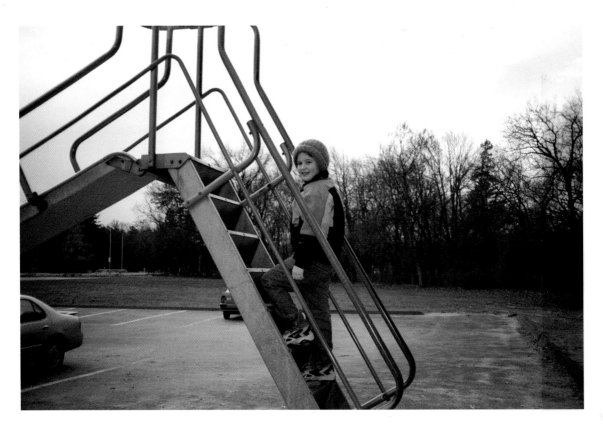

I am going up.

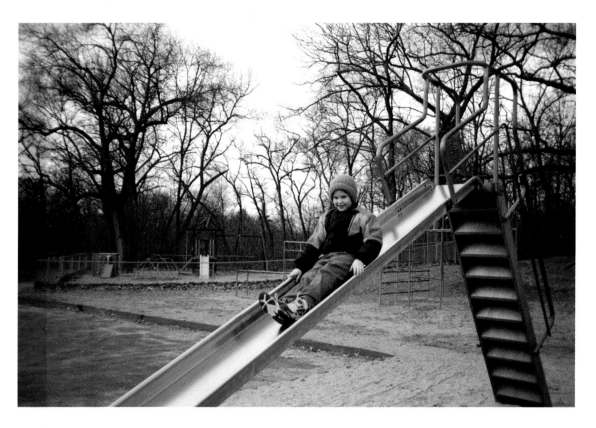

I am going down.

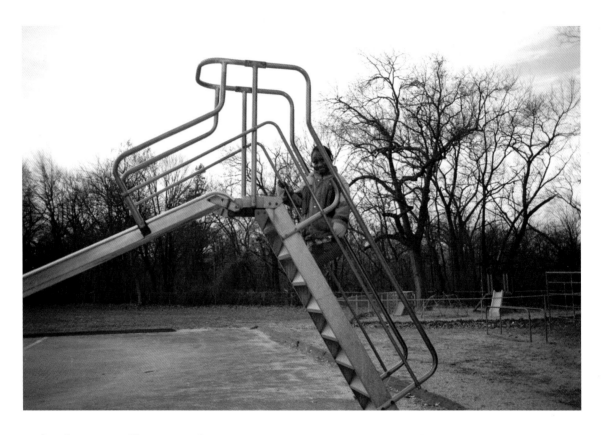

My friend is going up.

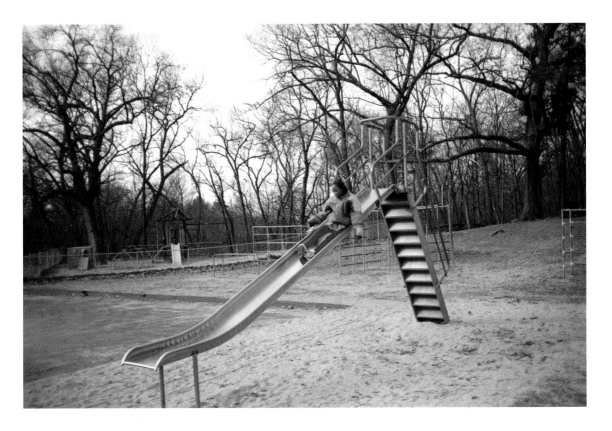

My friend is going down.

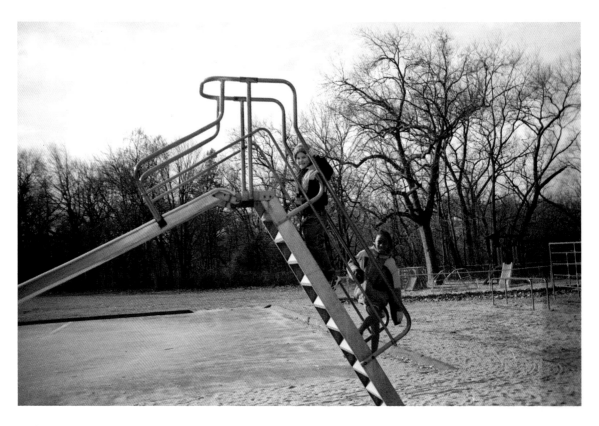

I am going up.
My friend is going up.

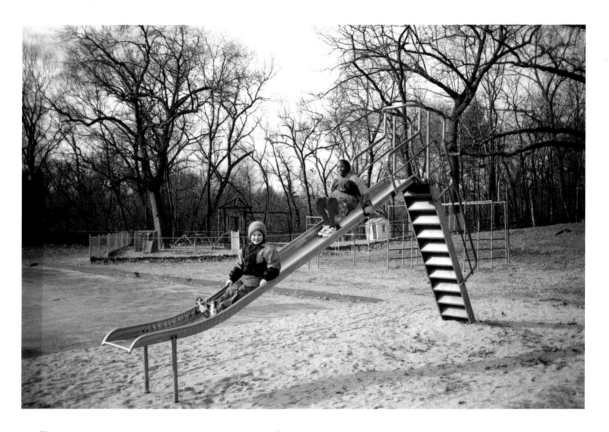

I am going down.
My friend is going down.

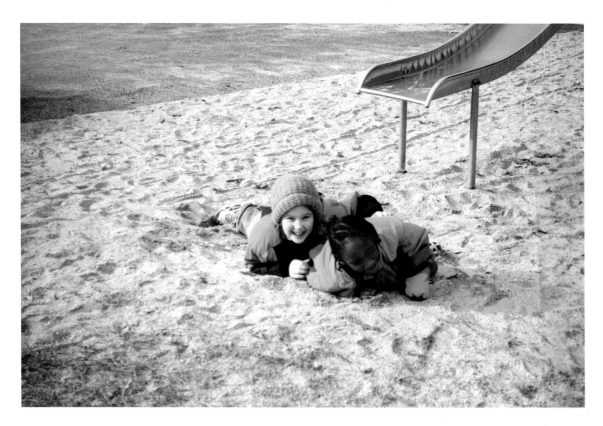

Crash!